BATAVIA PUBLIC LIBRARY DISTRICT

3 6173 00032 5608

P9-CCO-569

Jpb 90-02749
SCH 13.95
Schmid, Eleonore

Wake up, doormouse, Santa
Claus is here.

Withdrawn

BATAVIA PUBLIC LIBRARY
335 W. WILSON ST.
BATAVIA, ILLINOIS 60510
879-1393

LIBRARY CHARGES FOR
MISSING DATE CARD

To my sisters Silvia, Liselotte, and Verena

Jpb
Sc H

1. Christmas—fiction

Copyright © 1988 by Nord-Süd Verlag, Mönchaltorf, Switzerland.
First published in Switzerland under the title *Wach auf, Siebenschläfer, Sankt Nikolaus ist da.*
English translation copyright © 1989 by Elizabeth D. Crawford. North-South Books English
language edition copyright © 1989 by Rada Matija AG, 8625 Gossau ZH, Switzerland.

All rights reserved. No part of this book may be reproduced or utilized in any form
or by any means, electronic or mechanical, including photocopying, recording
or by any information storage and retrieval system, without permission in writing
from the Publisher. Printed in Italy. ISBN 1-55858-020-4

10 9 8 7 6 5 4 3 2 1

First published in the United States, Great Britain, Canada, Australia
and New Zealand in 1989 by North-South Books, an imprint of Rada Matija AG.

Library of Congress Catalog Card Number: 89-42610.

British Library Cataloguing in Publication Data

Schmid, Eleonore, *1939—*
    Wake up, dormouse, Santa Claus is here.
    I. Title II. Wach auf, Siebenschläfer,
    Sankt Nikolaus ist da. *English*
    833'.914 [J]

    ISBN 1-55858-020-4

90-02749

For a long time the woods rustled, fluttered, and snapped until
each animal and bird had settled into its own place again. Only
Gus the dormouse did not go home to his own nest. He had crept
into Santa Claus's pocket and happily fallen asleep there.

ELEONORE SCHMID

WAKE UP, DORMOUSE, SANTA CLAUS IS HERE

TRANSLATED BY ELIZABETH D. CRAWFORD

NORTH-SOUTH BOOKS NEW YORK

Gus lived all by himself in an old oak. Like everyone else in his family, he slept the whole day long, for he was a dormouse. Every night he woke up, stretched his legs, and crept out of his nest. Then he went looking for something to eat.

He needed to get round and fat so he wouldn't be hungry during
his long winter sleep. He looked for fruit, mushrooms, acorns,
and nuts. He gnawed sweet tree bark or hunted for insects. Whatever
he couldn't finish eating, he carried back to his nest for later.

In the fall, when the nights and days grew cool, Gus would curl up
in his nest like all the other dormice and sleep until spring. And so
every year Gus slept through the visit from Santa Claus. He only knew
of him from the stories he heard from the other animals in the forest.
This year Gus wanted to meet Santa Claus too, just for once in his life.

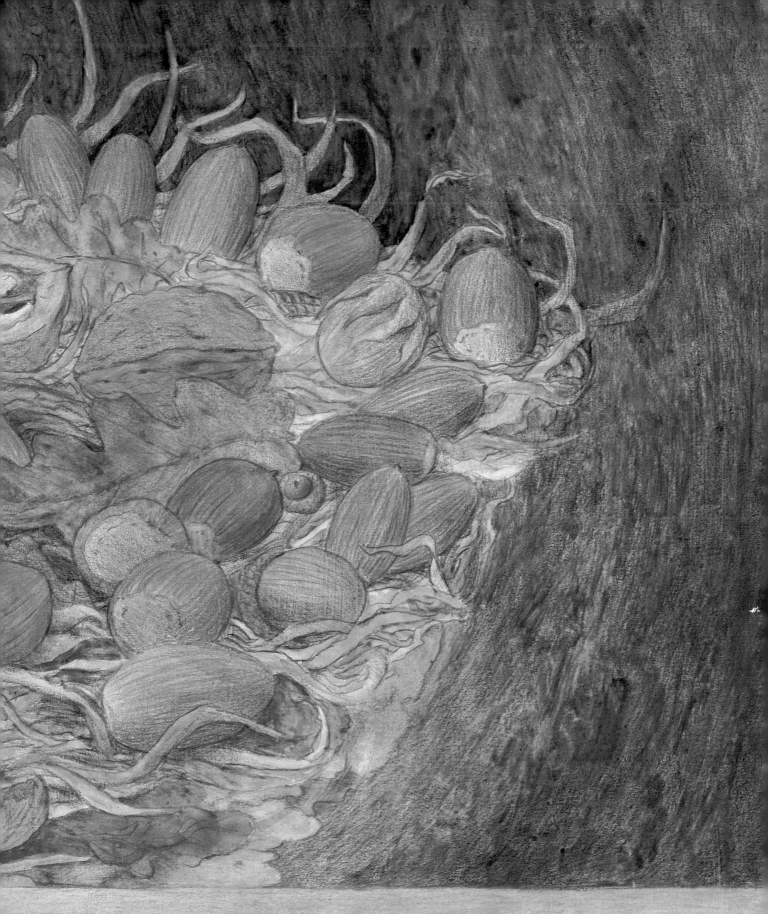

If only he knew how to keep awake! Maybe if he ate a little less... maybe if he just napped a little. He curled his tail tightly around himself, laid his paws on his tummy, closed his eyes and dreamed a quick dream....

"Ca-a-a-aw, ca-a-a-aw, humans coming," shrieked the crow on the branch nearby. Gus woke up suddenly. Was Santa Claus coming now? Carefully Gus stuck his head out of his hole and opened his sleepy eyes wide. A mother was gathering branches of

pine and mistletoe with her children. What did they want those for?
  Santa Claus wasn't there. Gus drew back into his snug hole in
the branch. He mustn't go to sleep again now, mustn't sleep,
mustn't. . . .

"Thrrr, thrrr, thrrr…" Gus was startled out of his sleep.
A woodpecker was boring a hole in the tree just above his nest.
"Has Santa Claus been here yet?" Gus asked quickly.
The woodpecker shook his head and kept on drilling.
"Do you know when he's coming?" Gus asked.

"When it's cold," the woodpecker replied.

But it's cold now! Gus thought as he crept back inside again.
A few withered leaves clung to the branches, and except for the
sound of the woodpecker, the forest was very, very quiet.

It was nearly dark. Something rustled on the ground. A squirrel
ran up the tree and begged Gus for an acorn.
"I can't find my food," he said, "and I'm hungry."
Gus gave him an acorn. "Have you seen Santa Claus?" he asked.
"I don't want to miss him this time. The other animals are awake

in the winter and get to see him but I'm always asleep and
don't know when he comes."

"I'll call you when Santa Claus comes," said the squirrel, and he
jumped down and bounded away.

An owl had been perched nearby. She heard everything.

Gus shivered. He snuggled down into his nest again. Outside it got colder and colder. The wind whistled and tore through the dry leaves. It shook the trees, but Gus didn't wake up.

One night the first snow fell. The fox was lurking in the bushes. He was hungry. Suddenly he pricked up his ears and sniffed. Then he saw a light at the edge of the forest. Joyfully he sprang forward.

Santa Claus was trudging through the snow with his donkey. With each step the little bells jingled, softly at first, then louder and louder. The animals in the forest had been waiting for this sound.

Santa Claus had come at last! As he entered a clearing in the
forest, all the animals came hopping, bounding, and flying to meet
him.

"Come, my friends," Santa said softly. "I have gifts for each of you."

Santa took a fat sack off the donkey's back and opened it. He pulled out carrots, red apples, and bread. The animals came closer, waiting for their food. On this moonlit winter night, no one was afraid of anyone else. Santa had brought sausage and a slab of

bacon for the foxes. For the birds he hung little bags of seed and fat on the branches and spread seed around on the ground. He gave nuts to the squirrels and cheese to the crow. The mice ran from one spot to another, nibbling on everything.

At last Santa Claus sat down wearily. "Have you all had enough?" he asked. "Did I forget anyone?"
The squirrel cocked his ears and waved his tail back and forth.

He had promised someone something, but now he had forgotten
what it was. Uneasily he looked from one animal to another.
Somewhere in the distance the owl hooted.

"Uhooo, uhoo, wake up, Gus, wake up!" The owl had to call several times before Gus woke up. "Come quickly," she said. "Santa Claus is here." Gus's legs were stiff. He stretched and yawned. He could barely get his eyes open.

How the forest had changed! The snow sparkled in the moonlight.
Gus had never seen so much white.
  "Follow me," called the owl, "I'll fly along ahead of you."
Gus felt as if he were in a dream as he leaped from branch to branch.

Santa Claus looked up the tree and stretched his arms up to Gus. The little dormouse's heart beat wildly. He jumped. Warm hands held him, and a friendly face was looking down at him.

"Gus! I was waiting for you. Now here you are with me," said

Santa Claus with a laugh as he stroked him gently. Then he fished in his pocket and gave him dried apples, pears, and plums. Gus nibbled contentedly. He was so happy.

It was very late. Santa Claus had to go on. He had a kind word
for each animal as he said good-bye. One after the other they
rubbed their heads against his shoulder and let him stroke them.
Then softly the animals left the clearing.